Grandma Comes to Stay Again

Written by Jill Eggleton

Illustrated by Kelvin Hawley

Rigby

The people in the book

Grandma

Kids

Dad

The house in the book

Dad's house

In the house

The garden

Grandma came to stay.
She had her birds.
She had her mice.
And she had her fish.

"The birds can't stay
in the cages,"
said Grandma.

She opened the cages
and the birds came out.

The birds will go...

on Dad's head?

on the fish bowl?

The birds sat on the chairs.
They sat on the table.
They sat on Dad's head!

"I don't like birds on my head," said Dad.

Grandma laughed.

"**The birds are happy,**" she said.

Grandma looked at the mice.

"The mice can't stay in the cages," she said.

She opened the cages and the mice came out.

The mice will go...

up Dad's pants?

up the curtain?

The mice ran up the table.
They ran up the chairs.
They ran up Dad's pants!

"Help!" shouted Dad.
"I don't like mice
up my pants!"

Grandma laughed and laughed!

The kids looked at the fish.

"The fish will have to stay in the bowls," they said.

"No they will not," said Grandma.

The fish will go...

in the bucket?

in the bathtub?

Grandma put water in the bathtub.

She put plants in the bathtub.

She put rocks in the bathtub.

And...

she put the fish in the bathtub!

"Oh, no," said Dad.
"Fish in my bathtub.
I don't like fish in my bathtub!"

Grandma looked at her birds and her mice and her fish.

"**Good**," she said.
"**They are all happy!**"

"**I am not happy,**" said Dad.
"**I can't stay in this house with birds and mice and fish in my bathtub!**"

Dad will go...

in the tent?

in the shed?

So the birds and the mice
and the fish
stayed in the house.

And Grandma and Dad and
the kids stayed in the tent.

Dad liked it.
No cooking.
The kids liked it.
No bath!

The End

Mapping charts

bedroom

bathroom

kitchen

bedroom

living room

Where can they go?

river

tree

pond

hole

sea

grass

nest

Word Bank

bathtub

mice

birds

plants

bowls

rocks

cages

table

chairs

tent

fish

water